THE HAMSTER WHO FELL TO EARTH

DANNY PEARSON

ILLUSTRATED BY SEB CAMAGAJEVAC

00237

Titles in Ignite II

Badger Publishing Limited
Oldmedow Road,
Hardwick Industrial Estate,
King's Lynn PE30 4JJ
Telephone: 01438 791037

www.badgerlearning.co.uk

2 4 6 8 10 9 7 5 3 1

The Hamster Who Fell to Earth ISBN 978-1-78147-449-5

Text © Danny Pearson 2013
Complete work © Badger Publishing Limited 2013

Publisher: Susan Ross
Senior Editor: Danny Pearson
Publishing Assistant: Jennifer Brough
Design: Fiona Grant
Illustration: Seb Camagajevac
Copyeditor: Ursula Faulkner

THE HAMSTER WHO FELL TO EARTH

Contents

Vocabulary:

amazement	cheerfully
crater	instantly
scurrying	spoilt
squeaked	stern

Main characters:

Nick

Lola

The hamster

Chapter 1

Crash!

It was late at night and Nick was fast asleep in bed when he was suddenly woken up by a loud crash. He sprang out of bed to look outside in the garden.

Nick could see that the shed had been flattened and smoke was coming from it. He raced downstairs and out into the garden for a closer look.

As he moved close to where the shed once stood, he could see that there was now a crater in the middle of it.

He slowly peered over into the crater, trying to clear the smoke away. To his surprise, he could see a small see-through ball with an even smaller ball of fur inside it.

"Nick! Nick! What is it? What's happened?" asked his dad who was also awake and being followed by Nick's mum and sister down the garden path.

"I don't know," replied Nick. "It must have come from the sky."

"What on earth are you talking about?" his dad asked as he reached Nick.

His dad, mum and sister all walked over the remains of the shed to look into the crater. They could now all see the small ball with an even smaller ball of fur inside it, too.

"Mummy, what is it?" asked Lola, Nick's sister.

"I don't know, sweetheart, ask your father," she answered.

"Search me," Nick's dad said as he scratched his head.

"I think I know," Nick said as he reached towards the ball. He gave it a gentle tap.

The ball of fur started to uncurl.

The rest of the family stood back. "Careful now, Nick," whispered his mum.

To their amazement, the small ball of fur gave out a little cough and they all instantly saw that it was a small hamster looking up at them.

"Awww, Mum, can we keep him!" shouted Lola. She had always wanted a pet.

"No way, you know your father can't stand fur."

"Your mother is right. This little thing must have got lost. First thing in the morning we shall call round the street to see if anyone has lost their pet," said Nick's dad in a stern voice.

"But, Dad, where did it come from and why is it wearing a little belt and jacket?" asked Nick.

His dad looked over the hamster in its ball a few more times. "It looks like one of those spoilt pets you see on the telly, where their owners dress them up in silly clothes."

"But, Dad, it looks like it crashed from the sky," snapped Nick.

"Nonsense," replied his dad. "Now off to bed, all of you, I will take care of this."

Chapter 2

Lost

The next morning a family meeting was called around the breakfast table.

Nick's dad stood up from his chair. "Now, I'm not sure what happened last night but there is someone out there who is missing their little beast."

"Dad, it's a hamster!" Lola called out.

"Quiet!" her dad ordered. "Now I want you and Nick to make a few 'lost' posters so we can put them up around the street and through people's letter boxes."

Nick thought that this was a stupid idea. No way had that hamster escaped from someone's house. He didn't think it was lost at all.

"Nick, will you be a dear and take a photo of it for the poster?" asked his mum.

Nick grabbed his camera and carried the hamster and its ball up to his room.

The hamster was again curled up in a ball asleep giving out little snores.

"Poor thing must be tired," thought Nick.

Nick took a few photos then he ran back downstairs, leaving the hamster in his room.

Nick helped his mum and sister to add the final touches to the 'lost' posters.

"Excellent work, we will have rid of this thing in no time," Nick's dad said with a smile on his face. "Now off you go and be sure to post it through everyone's letter boxes and put up as many as you can on post boxes, poles, fences… everything."

The family left the house, all with a stack of posters under each arm.

Chapter 3

Hello

"Well, that was a waste of time," sighed Nick, as the family walked back into their house.

They had spent the last five hours, knocking door to door, checking to see if anyone had lost their hamster.

No one was missing a hamster and Nick's dad had even tried to give the hamster away to a nice elderly couple that lived across the street.

"So, Dad, do we get to keep him?" asked Lola with a sweet look on her face.

"NO! That thing is not staying here. My eyes are starting to water from its fur," her dad said with tears in his eyes.

Nick rolled his eyes. "Fine, I will go and check on it, come on Lola."

They went upstairs to Nick's room.

As they walked into his room they could see the ball laying on the floor open, with no hamster in it.

"Oh, no, he's escaped," Lola said tearfully.

Then they heard tapping and both of them turned to Nick's computer.

To their amazement, they could see that the hamster was busy typing away on the keyboard. Their jaws dropped.

The hamster quickly looked over. "Hello," it said. "My name is Han, pleased to meet you."

Lola jumped up and down. "He talks, he talks!"

Nick quickly shut the bedroom door behind him. "You can talk?"

"Yes, yes, I can. I see you can too, this is good news," it said cheerfully. "Now, I was wondering if you could show me how to get here." Han the hamster pointed to the computer screen.

Nick and Lola raced over to see what he was pointing at.

"You want to go to the garden centre, why?" Nick quizzed.

"Yes, I do. You see I do a bit of gardening and there is an intergalactic flower show on soon and I do love the flowers you have here on Earth. I am bound to win first prize if I can get my paws on a few seeds."

"Let's help him, let's get him some seeds," Lola said excitedly.

"OK, sure thing. We can take you there; it's just down the road."

Chapter 4

Found

"We are just off to the garden centre, we are taking Han… I mean the hamster with us!" Nick called out to his parents.

"OK, have fun!" their mum called back, who was now applying eye drops to their dad's eyes.

Nick and Lola made their way out of the house with the hamster in his ball.

When they reached the garden centre Han was delighted. He was scurrying up and down the aisles in his little ball.

"Amazing!" he squeaked. "I have never seen such a collection! Please help me gather them."

"Erm, OK, but we do have to pay for these you know," said Nick.

"Oh, yes, you use money on this planet, don't you? Well, let me see what I have."

Han reached into a pocket on his belt and pulled out a gold nugget. "Will this do?"

Nick quickly grabbed it, "Yep, that will do."

They carried on shopping, filling up the hamster's ball full of different types of seeds.

Meanwhile, a car had pulled up outside their house. Three large men got out and knocked on the family's door.

Nick's dad answered. "Hello, gentlemen, can I help?"

One of them took off his sunglasses. "Yes, we believe you can. Did an object by any chance land in your garden last night?"

Nick's dad gulped, "I don't know about landed but we found a hamster in its exercise ball."

One of the men took out a radio. "We have located the visitor."

The other men moved closer. "Where exactly is this hamster, sir?"

Nick's mum had now come to the door. "What is going on here?" she asked.

"Honey, these gentlemen want to know where that hamster is." Nick's dad said through a fake smile.

"Oh, the kids took it to the local garden centre. I haven't got a clue what they are going to do there but I am sure they are having fun," she answered.

The three men looked at each other then ran back to their car and drove off.

Nick's mum shut the door. "Well, they were odd, cup of tea, dear?"

Chapter 5

A message

Nick, Lola and Han were having a great time. Han's ball was now so full that he was pressed up against the side.

"Thank you so much for all your help, I am done here now. Could you please attach the ship's hatch for me?"

Nick's eyes lit up. "You mean the top of your exercise ball?"

The hamster looked up with a puzzled look. "No, this is my ship. Please could you put the hatch back on so I can get back home."

Nick smiled and kneeled down to screw the top back on. "I knew it!"

Just then, the three large men came running into the garden centre. "Stop that creature!" one of them yelled.

"Oops, time for me to go," Han said.

With one loud squeak the ball lifted from the ground. "Thank you again for your help, I will be sure to let you know how I get on."

The men raced over to where they were. One of them dived over a stack of flower pots to try and grab the ship.

Han squeaked again and the ball shifted out of the way.

The man landed on the floor, and with one last loud squeak the ball flew high up into the sky.

Lola jumped up and down with excitement, clapping her hands.

Six weeks later…

Things were a lot quieter since Han left and no one was given any explanation as to who, or what, had crashed into their shed.

"Family meeting!" called Nick's dad.

Everyone slowly made their way round the breakfast table.

Nick's dad stood up. "Now, I'm not sure what happened a few weeks ago but people are starting to think we are crazy because Lola will not stop talking about flying hamsters… "

Just then, the TV turned itself on.

"It's Han! It's Han!" cried out Lola.

Han was at the intergalactic flower show. "Hello, everybody, I just wanted to say thank you again for helping me. I am pleased to report, that with your help, I won first prize!"

Hamsters

Hamsters found here on Earth are part of the rodent family.

There are more than 25 species of hamsters ranging from the European breed measuring up to 13.4 in (34 cm) long to the tiny dwarf hamsters with bodies of 2 to 4 inches (5.5 to 10.5 cm) long.

In the wild, they spend most of the day underground trying to avoid being caught by predators. They eat seeds, fruits, and will sometimes even eat small insects.

They have big cheek pouches that they are able to store food in. When full, the cheeks can make their heads double, or even triple, in size.

Hamsters have poor eyesight and are colorblind, but they do have a very good sense of smell and can hear very high-pitched noises.

They usually come out at night and their large eyes help them to see better in dark conditions.

Hamsters use their whiskers to help detect objects and to explore. The whiskers vibrate backwards and forwards at rates of up to 30 times per second.

The lifespan of a hamster depends on its breed. Dwarf hamsters usually live between two to three years. While the larger breeds can sometimes live until the ripe old age of four years.

The best-known type of hamster is the golden, or Syrian hamster, which is the type most commonly kept as pets.

Questions

Where does Nick and his family find the hamster?

What does the hamster look like?

What is its name and what was it looking at on Nick's computer?

Who do you think the three men are that are looking for the hamster?

How does the hamster escape from the three men?

What can the family see on the TV in the last chapter?

What would you do if an alien landed in your garden?